MW01045538

OF HOME
AND HEART

ANNE SCHRAFF

Artesian Press

P.O. Box 355, Buena Park, CA 90621

STANDING TALL MYSTERY SERIES
MULTICULTURAL READERS
SET 3

Project Editor: Molly Mraz
Illustrator: Fujiko
Graphic Design: Tony Amaro
©2003 Artesian Press

Artesian **Press**

ISBN 1-58659-105-3

CONTENTS

Chapter 1

Eighteen-year-old Bijan Haji was working at the computer, trying to find out more about the Big Bang theory, when he heard a crash. The whole house seemed to shudder from the force of something hitting the west wall.

"What was that?" Bijan's mother cried out in terror.

Bijan's sixteen-year-old brother, Waseel, ran toward the front door. "Sounds like it came from next door. Those creeps are at it again," Waseel said.

But before he could grab the doorknob, Mother was clutching his arm, holding him back. "Don't go over there, Waseel! Please don't. I don't want any trouble!" she said.

"It's those little brats over there bothering us again, Ma. They ripped up the flowers from your garden. They rode their bicycles over our lawn. Now they're throwing rocks at our house! Why can't we call the police?" Waseel asked angrily.

Now Neheda Haji looked really frightened. "The police? Never! When I was a little girl, the police took my brother away, and I never saw him again! I want nothing to do with police!" she said.

"Ma," Waseel groaned, "that was in Iraq! We've been in the United States for five years!"

Bijan wished his father was home, but he hardly ever was. He owned the deli at the corner of the street, and he worked sixteen to eighteen hours a day. Bijan and Waseel often worked there, too. Bijan didn't mind. The family was making some money. They already had a nice little house. The future looked good.

Bijan waited a few minutes until his mother had gone into the kitchen. Then he stepped outside. He found a cantaloupe-sized rock lying at the side of the house. Bijan shook his head sadly. Why were those two middle-school boys next door so mean? They started out riding their bicycles across the Haji's lawn. Then Jeff, the thirteen-year-old, threw a baseball through the kitchen window. Bijan's father yelled at them, but they just acted worse after that.

Bijan saw Jeff Tomlinson tossing a basketball at the garage door hoop. "Hey, Jeff, that wasn't very nice of you to throw that rock at our house. You upset my ma," Bijan said.

Jeff stopped bouncing the basketball. He stared at Bijan. "I didn't throw any rock," he said.

"A big rock just hit our house, and it came from the direction of your house," Bijan said. He couldn't figure out why the Tomlinsons hated his family—unless maybe they hated Iraqis, or maybe *all* immigrants.

"I didn't throw the rock," Jeff said. "Somebody could have thrown it from the alley. How come you're always blaming me for stuff? You're foreigners and I'm an American. You can't yell at me. Why don't you go back to Iraq?"

"We're Americans, too," Bijan said. "We're citizens now. I saw you throw that baseball that broke our kitchen window that day, and you denied that, too, Jeff."

"It was an accident. I was scared of your old man. He's a really mean guy. He acted like I killed somebody or something. You people have got a lot of nerve, trying to act like you're so important," Jeff said. His brother, Bobby, came from the house and stood beside Jeff. Bobby was twelve.

"You shut up, Bijan!" Bobby screamed. "We hate you! You leave my brother alone. He didn't do anything!"

"My dad says you people should get out and go back to where you came from," Jeff said. Then he and his brother went inside their house, slamming the door. Bijan had a sick feeling in the pit of his stomach.

Chapter 2

Waseel joined Bijan outside. "What did he say?" he asked. "What did Jeff Tomlinson say? I heard you talking to him."

"He says he didn't throw the rock," Bijan said. "And he said we should all go back to Iraq."

Waseel made a face. "The little liar! He and his family should move somewhere else if they don't like us."

"I wish there was some way to get through to those people," Bijan said. "We can't go on like this. They're our closest neighbors."

"Yeah, maybe we could invite them all over for some of Ma's *baklava*," Waseel said. "That's how it works in the fairy tales right? The mean old neighbor comes and eats some pie, and he's sweet as sugar after all. Only this is the real world."

"We got off to a bad start with them," Bijan said. "And Dad yelled at the boys a lot when they broke the window."

"I'm glad he did," Waseel said. "I wish we could call the police and get those kids arrested. Ma's wrong about the police. Most of them are okay here."

As the boys stood talking, Bijan noticed the curtains in the Tomlinson's window open. Ned Tomlinson, Jeff and Bobby's father, was staring out. Even from this distance, in the dusk, you could see the anger in his face.

In his astronomy class at the community college the next day, Bijan sat in his usual place beside Samiya Askar, a very pretty girl who was also from Iraq. She wasn't Bijan's girlfriend, but she was a friend. Bijan had a lot of different friends—Hispanic, Asian, black, and white kids— but he liked Samiya because she reminded him of home.

Both Bijan and Samiya came from the same small village near Mosul in Iraq. It was a very poor farming community, but the people were very close to each other. The Haji family left the village five years earlier, but Samiya and her family had just moved here. She was still very homesick.

Bijan was almost thirteen when he left Iraq, and he remembered playing with Samiya, who was twelve. She had huge, shining dark eyes. Bijan often thought he could love her, but even then she liked a tall boy named Faisel.

"Those nasty neighbors of ours threw a rock at our house last night," Bijan told Samiya.

"They are no different from most of the people here," Samiya said angrily. "I wish we had never come here."

"Samiya, you know that's not true," Bijan said. "I've got lots of good friends. You know most people aren't like the Tomlinsons."

Samiya continued to look angry. "You are foolish, Bijan. You are one of those silly Polly . . . Polly—" Samiya spoke good English, but sometimes she struggled with an unfamiliar word.

"Pollyanna?" Bijan said.

"Yes, that's it. Those silly people who see good when there is no good. Just because some of the kids talk nice to you, you think they like you, but they don't. They don't like us. Just because I wear a scarf over my hair, they make fun of me when they think I'm not looking. I see them. I see them all the time laughing at me," Samiya said.

"They're just curious because most girls don't cover their hair around here," Bijan said.

"Ha!" Samiya said. "I know how they look at your own mother with her long, dark dresses and her covered head. They think, 'oh look, there goes another of those weird people. What are they doing here anyway?' They want us to be like them, exactly like them. They want everybody to look the same, or they bother us and make fun of us."

Bijan was shocked by the bitterness in Samiya's voice. He knew she missed her homeland—especially the boy she left behind—but he didn't know she was this upset. He felt sorry for her.

Chapter 3

Before the astronomy professor arrived, Samiya leaned over toward Bijan. "I was at the mall the other day with my cousin," she said. "These boys came along. They laughed out loud at us, and this one boy with funny hair said, 'what are you—witches?'"

"Samiya, just because a few people are stupid," Bijan started to say. Then the professor came in. Mr. Chen started the class immediately. Bijan looked around the room. It seemed that most of the students were from Asia, Africa, or Hispanic countries. Only about one-third of them were from European countries.

Everybody seemed to get along just fine. Bijan felt very comfortable here. But now he began to worry. Maybe Samiya was right. Maybe he did not see what was right in front of him. After all, the Tomlinsons certainly hated his family!

Bijan had lunch that day with his best friend, Elie Jacobs, a Jewish boy. Bijan and Elie started an astronomy club because they both loved the planets, stars, and galaxies. They hoped to eventually buy a good telescope that the club members could use.

"Man, Mr. Chen was great today," Elie said. "He made the Big Bang theory really clear."

"Yeah," Bijan said.

Elie was grinning from the lecture. "Like he says, 'All the earth's matter was in this big glob and then—pow! It all goes flying off in every direction and we have the solar system and galaxies—everything.'"

"Yeah, he's good," Bijan said.

"Hey, man, what's wrong? You don't seem like yourself," Elie said.

Bijan told him about the rock-throwing incident from last night.

"Are those the same fools who've been bothering you?" Elie asked.

"Yeah, the Tomlinsons. I guess they hate Iraqis or something. This kid Jeff said his father told him we should all get out of the country," Bijan said.

"You don't have to take stuff like that, Bijan," Elie said. "Your father should talk to the parents of those kids, and if they won't stop, call the police."

"My mother is scared to do that. She remembers what the police were like back home. You didn't want to get them mixed up in your life. They were worse than the criminals," Bijan said.

"Hey, you've got to forget about all that, Bijan. I mean, my own grandparents lived when Hitler ruled Germany, but I don't see my grandma looking for Hitler behind the trees in the park. This is the United States, right?" Elie said.

The two boys went to their next

classes, but all during the day Bijan was thinking about what Samiya had said. He found himself staring at other students and wondering if the warm smiles they gave him were real.

Maybe, Bijan thought, *it was harder for a girl than a guy*. If you were a girl from Iraq, you wore a covering on your head and so you looked different. The boys from Iraq looked like everybody else.

In the last class of the day, history, Samiya sat in front of Bijan. A good-looking, well-built boy sat next to her. Bijan never paid any attention to the boy before, but now he noticed that the boy was looking at Samiya.

Class hadn't started yet. The boy suddenly asked Samiya, "Do you have to always wear that thing?"

Samiya sat up straight. Bijan could see her shoulders stiffen. "What?" she asked.

"Over your hair. You've got nice hair. I can see it peeking out from under the scarf," the guy said. He reached out his hand towards Samiya's hair.

Samiya shrank away. "Don't touch me!" she cried in a trembling voice. Then she turned and looked back at Bijan, as if asking for help.

Chapter 4

"Hey, just leave her alone," Bijan said. He didn't say it in a mean way.

The guy turned, anger in his eyes. "Who are you, her boyfriend or something?"

"No," Bijan said, "just a friend. Calm down."

"What's the matter with her?" the guy asked. "Is she crazy? I wasn't going to do anything."

Samiya got up, grabbed her purse, and ran out of the classroom. The teacher was just coming in, but Bijan could not leave Samiya out there by herself as upset as she was.

So Bijan went to the teacher's desk and said, "I'll be right back. A friend of mine had to leave class because she wasn't feeling well."

The teacher nodded, and Bijan went out to search for Samiya. He found her sitting on a bench, crying.

"Samiya, are you okay?" Bijan asked.

"No!" she said. "I will never be okay in this country. I want to go home. I want to go back to our village. I hate it here. I hate everybody here. You saw that boy just now—what he did."

"Samiya, he was a jerk for trying to touch your hair, but he didn't mean—" Bijan started to say.

"Again, Pollyanna," Samiya said bitterly. "I get letters from Faisel. He warns me about American guys. He is so worried about me."

Bijan convinced Samiya to return to the classroom, but this time she sat in the back row, far from the boy who had bothered her. Bijan thought Samiya's biggest problem was that the move to the United States had separated her from the boy she loved. Everything else was affected by her loneliness for the boy.

Bijan had bought an old used car this past summer, and it came in handy getting him to and from school. After classes, he hurried toward his car and was about to get in when he noticed a folded piece of paper under the windshield wiper.

When Bijan unfolded the paper and read the message, he was shocked.

"Go home, Iraqi. We don't want you here."

Bijan stood there, stunned. Nothing like this had ever happened to him before. He looked around, wondering if someone from the college had done this. The Tomlinson boys went to the middle school just down the street from the community college. Maybe one of them had come over here and put the hate message on his car. They knew what his car looked like. But would they go that far?

Then Bijan remembered the guy in history class. He was probably the one who did it. He was so angry that Bijan interrupted his conversation with Samiya. Maybe he was trying to scare Bijan.

As Bijan looked around, he noticed another Iraqi student taking the same sort of paper from under his windshield wiper. Everybody at school knew Sami. He was one of the editors for the school newspaper. He was always telling people about Iraq being the birthplace of civilization. He was a little bit too proud.

"Hey, Sami, did you get one, too?" Bijan called to him.

"Yeah. I think they want me to go home," Sami said. "Unfortunately for them, I am not going." He was treating the note as a joke. Sami was like that. Nothing got him angry. "Never got one of these before though."

"I've never gotten one, either," Bijan said. He looked around, thinking he might see a suspicious person hanging around. He looked at every strange face now as a possible enemy. It was a terrible feeling. He never had it before, and he was sad. He didn't want to feel this way, but how could he feel any other way now?

Chapter 5

Bijan did not want to tell his mother about the note, but he talked to his father about it that evening at the deli.

"You think it's some kind of joke?" Father asked.

"I don't know. At first I thought the Tomlinson kids had done it. I'm not sure though," Bijan said. "There was a note on Sami's car, too. How would those kids know he was from Iraq?"

"They are hateful people," Father said. "They play their radio real loud and they listen to this guy who is always saying that there are too many immigrants in this country," Father said. "I wouldn't be surprised if those boys went around the school parking lot and stuck their notes on cars they recognized. Sami is always driving around in that red car. Maybe they have seen him."

"Maybe," Bijan said. He took over the deli while his father went to get a haircut. The customers were mostly Hispanics and blacks, and they were all nice and friendly. Two blonde girls came in, and they were nice, too. Bijan thought maybe he had been right in the first place. There was only a small minority of hate-filled people around here. He felt better.

Close to seven o'clock, Bijan's mother came in with Waseel.

There were a half a dozen people in the store looking around as Mother and Waseel restocked some of the shelves. The whole family had to help from time to time to keep things going.

Waseel joined Bijan behind the counter then. He said in a soft voice, "I wish Ma wouldn't dress like that."

"Why? What's the problem?" Bijan asked.

Waseel shrugged. "You know. It makes her look so different. She would look like anybody else if she'd just . . . " He stopped talking and just shook his head.

Bijan felt sorry for his sixteen-year-old brother. Waseel didn't have a car yet, and Mother picked him up at school. Some of his high school classmates probably had made some remarks. He was embarrassed.

"It's not important," Bijan said. "If Ma feels comfortable dressing like that, it's her business. She's not bothering anybody."

"Yeah, I know," Waseel said, "but there's this girl in my class—Jenny. We sort of like each other. But when she sees Ma, she always makes these little jokes, and it bothers me a lot."

"She shouldn't do that," Bijan said.

"I know," Waseel said, "but Ma does look weird. I mean, Ma is a pretty lady and she'd look good in regular clothes like all the women wear. She doesn't have to dress like some old lady . . . "

"Samiya and her cousins wear scarves, and they're young," Bijan said. "They aren't ashamed."

"But nobody else dresses like that here," Waseel said. "Why do we have to look so different?"

"Hey, Waseel, just because we're Americans now doesn't mean we have to give up our way of life. If Ma and Samiya feel comfortable dressing like they do, covering their heads in public, I don't see why they can't do it. I mean, it's kind of like a mark of respect for a girl or a woman to cover her head," Bijan said.

"You don't care," Waseel said in a bitter voice. "Ma isn't picking you up at school with all the kids staring and laughing."

"Not all the kids, Waseel, just a few jerks," Bijan said.

Just then, Samiya's cousin came running into the deli. She was very upset. "Samiya's been hurt!" she screamed.

"Right at the end of the street. Call an ambulance. Oh! Please hurry!"

Chapter 6

Bijan's parents stood together wondering what could have happened as an ambulance raced down the street to pick up Samiya. The Askar family lived in an apartment complex on the next street.

The details of the attack on Samiya weren't clear at first. All kinds of wild rumors were heard throughout the neighborhood.

Then, just before ten o'clock that night, Samiya's mother called the Haji house. Bijan's mother spoke with her.

Bijan listened to his mother's end of the conversation.

"Ah, good," Mother said, "then she is all right. Yes, yes, that is a good idea—to keep her overnight in the hospital. Just to be sure. She must have been so frightened. Her cousins are with her now? Oh, good. What a terrible thing. I know, I know . . ."

When Mother hung up the phone she told her family what had happened to Samiya.

"Some boys were following her in an automobile. She was walking on the sidewalk, and they were yelling insults at her. She ignored them at first, but then they stopped the car. They grabbed her and pulled off her scarf. It was dark. She did not see their faces. How foolish it was for her to walk home alone in the dark. Maybe in our village at home, but not here. The boys smashed rotten tomatoes in Samiya's hair . . . and who knows what else they were going to do, but she got away. She ran and fell and cut her knee . . . then they drove off."

Bijan listened in shock. Who would do such a thing? The boy in history class and his friends? Would he be that evil?

"Is Samiya sure she didn't see their faces?" Bijan asked.

"The car windows were dark, so she could not look in, and when they stopped, they came at her from behind. She said she was so frightened, she didn't remember seeing anything," Mother said.

"What do the police say?" Father asked.

"Oh, they did not call the police. They told the ambulance people that Samiya fell and hurt herself. They said nothing about the boys," Mother said.

"But that is not right," Father shouted. "It was a brutal attack and those boys must be punished!"

"Samiya cannot bear to talk about it," Mother said. "Who knows what happened? Her mother said she was crying for hours. She began to scream when her father mentioned the police. She is such a sensitive girl. They had to give her some medicine to calm her down. Poor Samiya. I understand how she feels.

How could she describe what those boys did to the police? They would probably laugh at her."

"No, they wouldn't laugh at her," Bijan said. "Like Pa says, it's wrong not to call the police."

Mother's face looked angry. "Respect the poor girl's feelings. That is what I say. Men do not understand such things. Those terrible boys touching her. It is cruel to make her talk about it. Besides, they will never catch the boys. Why should the poor girl have to tell her story over and over? She is not seriously hurt. Her family can be thankful for that. I told her mother that Samiya must not walk alone at night, ever."

Samiya did not return to classes at the community college for the next three days. When she did finally go back on Friday morning, she looked at Bijan and said in a bitter voice, "Well, what do you say now? Do you now admit this is a bad and evil place we have come to? Didn't I tell

you, Bijan? But you would not believe it.
Maybe you believe it now. Maybe now
you will stop being the Pollyanna?"

Chapter 7

Elie Jacobs came along as Bijan and Samiya were talking. "Hey, Samiya, you okay? There's talk about you being hurt."

"Some creeps threw rotten tomatoes at me and stuff, but I don't want to talk about it," Samiya said.

"Why would anybody do that?" Elie asked.

"Because they hate me," Samiya said. "They hate people from the Middle East, people who dress differently than they do."

"Hey, I don't believe that," Elie said. "I got friends from Sudan, and they dress much differently. We go eat at their house and they come to our place. Everybody in the neighborhood goes to the Haji deli.

They all like Bijan's dad. Maybe you hurt some jerk's feelings or something, Samiya."

"This creep tried to pull my scarf off in history class. Maybe he was responsible for what happened," Samiya said. "I don't care. It's all part of the awful things that keep happening to us around here. I hate it here." With that Samiya walked away.

Elie stood there shaking his head.

"There has been other stuff happening to Iraqi kids," Bijan said. "I told you about the rock that hit our house and then those notes pinned to my windshield and Sami's, too."

"You need to go to the police, man," Elie said.

"I can't. Ma would be really frightened if the police showed up to talk to me. And I can't tell the police what happened to Samiya if she wants to keep it secret," Bijan said.

"Look, Bijan, there's this cop who bowls with my dad, Sergeant Jackson.

He's pretty cool. You can tell stuff to him and he checks it out unofficially, you know what I mean? Like some girl's ex-boyfriend was bothering her, so Jackson had a serious talk with the guy, off the record. You and he should get together," Elie said.

"I don't know, Elie. He might think we're weird people, too. My own *brother* is ashamed of the way Ma dresses!" Bijan said.

"No, he won't think you're weird," Elie said. "His wife and daughters dress like Samiya and your Mom."

"You mean he's from the Middle East, too?" Bijan asked.

"No, no," Elie laughed. "He was born right here in L.A. His name is Kwame Jackson, and he's a Black Muslim. My dad likes him a lot, and my dad is kind of a grump. If you can get along with my dad, you must be okay."

"You sure he won't report what I tell him and start some big investigation?"

Bijan asked.

"You can trust the guy, man. I wouldn't lie to you. Look, you and I have to stick together. When somebody is bothering you, they're bothering me. You and I have to keep the astronomy club going and get that telescope. I can't have you worrying about people who hate for no good reason," Elie said.

The following afternoon after classes at the college, Bijan and Sgt. Jackson met at a sandwich shop. Jackson was a big, mahogany-colored man. He looked very scary until he smiled. Then you could tell that he was really a nice man.

"So, Bijan. Elie Jacobs tells me some guys are giving you a hard time. Maybe we got some hate crimes going on."

Bijan told Sgt. Jackson everything that had happened. Then he said, "But my mother doesn't want the police to know. The girl I told you about doesn't, either. If you could just sort of check it out unofficially . . . "

"I understand," Sgt. Jackson said, smiling. "I'll see what I can do."

Chapter 8

Before he left, Bijan could not help asking Sgt. Jackson, "Uh, Elie says your family—I mean, your wife and daughters wear scarves and stuff . . . "

Sgt. Jackson grinned again. "You bet. I don't want my girls dressing like most of these young ladies in the neighborhood. No way. I see these girls in short skirts and tiny tops, and I get nervous. I want my daughters to get some respect."

Bijan felt better now that he told somebody in authority what was going on. He wasn't sure if it would do any good, but he was relieved. It was scary having all kinds of bad things happening and keeping them secret.

Bijan was studying in the library the

following day when a dark shadow fell across the book he was reading.

When he looked up, he saw the boy from history class who had frightened Samiya.

"I need to talk to you," the boy said. "There's talk going around that maybe I attacked some Iraqi girl."

"I didn't hear anything like that," Bijan said.

"Some of the guys in history class are saying that girl I tried to talk to the other day got messed up and maybe I did it."

"No," Bijan said, trying to sound innocent.

"Look, she's a pretty girl. I thought she just wore that scarf like a fashion thing. I didn't know she was one of those women who have to wear something over their heads. When she got so upset and you acted like the big hero, saving her from a monster . . . " he said, anger in his voice.

"I just didn't want her upset," Bijan

said.

"I'm on the football team. Look, if the coach hears about something like this, I could get kicked off the team, you know?" the boy went on.

"I don't think anybody blames you for anything," Bijan said.

"Yeah? That's not what I'm hearing. You people have these real strange ideas, and you think it's some major crime to just look at a girl or something." The boy's eyes were dark with anger. "I'm not going to be ruined over this, you know? I've been in a little bit of trouble before over some stupid fraternity party, and this is all I need to get kicked out for good."

"I don't even know your name," Bijan said.

"Frost. Toby Frost," the boy said. "Remember that name. If a bunch of weirdos accuse me of something I didn't do, well, you guys are going to be sorry you ever heard the name Frost. Because I'm not taking this without a fight, okay?"

"Nobody is accusing you of anything," Bijan said. He tried to keep his voice calm, but inside he was far from calm. Toby Frost looked like a volcano getting ready to erupt. When he finally waked off, Bijan took a deep breath. He had been so nervous he even forgot to breathe for a few seconds.

Bijan closed the book he was reading. All of a sudden the Big Bang theory in space did not seem as important as what was about to happen right here on earth.

Bijan met Elie in the coffee shop across the street after classes. Many college kids went there because there were lumpy old sofas and overstuffed chairs to sit in while you drank your coffee and just relax.

"Did you get to talk to Sgt. Jackson?" Elie asked.

"Yeah, I liked him. Thanks for telling me about him, Elie," Bijan said. "Hey, do you know anything about a guy named Toby Frost? He sort of gave Samiya a hard time the other day, but I didn't even know his name then."

Elie got a look on his face that scared Bijan. "Yeah, I know him," he said, "he's a bad guy."

Chapter 9

"So tell me," Bijan said nervously.

"He was dating this high school girl last year and she broke up with him. He got so mad, he tricked her into coming to a fraternity party. He and his buddies really teased her and were mean to her all night. The fraternity was suspended for six months and Frost almost got kicked out of college. His father had to write a check to the college to save him," Elie said.

"If he got that angry over a girl breaking up with him, then maybe he *is* the guy who hurt Samiya," Bijan said.

"It's possible," Elie said, finishing his cup of black coffee. "He's a creep, that's for sure. But don't assume that's what happened. Like my pop says, when you assume things, you get into more trouble."

Two girls were sitting across from Bijan and Elie. Bijan recognized them from his English class, Alyssa and Judith. Bijan liked Alyssa. A few times he even thought about asking her out, but something always stopped him. Now, when she saw him looking at her, she smiled.

In a minute, the girls came over with their coffee. "You're Mexican, aren't you?" Alyssa asked Bijan.

"No," Bijan said.

"Oh, you're kind of dark, so I thought you were Mexican," Alyssa said.

"Tall, dark, and handsome," Judith giggled.

Bijan felt his face get warm. He was flattered that the girls liked him. But he wondered if they still would if they knew where he was from. He decided to take a chance.

"I'm from Iraq," he said.

"Oh," Alyssa said. Bijan studied her

face. Was she disappointed that he wasn't Mexican? Would she dislike him because he was Iraqi? He tried to see how she felt by looking in her eyes, but he couldn't tell. She kept on smiling. "How long have you been in the United States?" she asked him finally.

"A little more than five years," Bijan said. "I was almost thirteen when we came here. I liked the music right away. Everything else was hard to get used to, but I sure liked the music. You're probably going to laugh, but I love country rock."

Alyssa's smile got bigger. "I'm a bluegrass fan! Isn't that the weirdest thing? All my friends like rock, but I just love bluegrass," she said.

"Hey," Bijan said impulsively, "there's a country bluegrass festival this weekend, on Saturday. Want to go?"

"You bet," Alyssa said, scribbling her phone number on a paper and giving it to Bijan.

"I'll call you," Bijan promised.

As the girls walked away laughing, Elie turned to Bijan and said, "Cool, man. You're good."

"Yeah, I guess she likes me," Bijan said.

"Well, you're not too bad looking," Elie said.

Bijan laughed. "It's just that with all that's been happening I've been thinking maybe Samiya is right, that most of the kids hate us," he said.

"Most people are fair," Elie said. "They give you a chance."

Bijan was starting to get up when he saw Toby Frost come into the coffee shop. Frost stood in the doorway looking around.

"Uh-oh," Bijan muttered. Frost seemed to be looking for somebody.

"Coach Landers heard what's been happening!" Toby Frost yelled. "I need to talk to that girl with the scarf. She's been saying bad things about me, I know it. I don't even know her name, and she's trying to get me in trouble. You're one of her people—so tell me, who is she, and where can I find her?"

Chapter 10

Bijan felt cold. Did this jerk really think Bijan was going to send him to Samiya's door?

"Come on, man. I need to stop this girl from spreading lies about me," Toby Frost said.

"I don't know where she lives," Bijan said.

"You're a liar. You people all know each other," Frost said angrily.

"I'm leaving," Bijan said, walking toward the door.

He and Elie were riding in Elie's pickup today, so they hurried to the parking lot where they left it.

"He'll probably try to follow us," Bijan said. "He figures we're going to warn

Samiya that he's after her."

"We do need to warn her," Elie said. "But if he's following us, we'll find another way to get there."

The boys jumped into the pickup and drove off. As they drove down the street, nobody seemed to be following them. Bijan breathed a sigh of relief.

Around six-thirty, the boys drove to Samiya's apartment complex. A number of Iraqi families lived there. Samiya lived with her parents and two brothers. The brothers were both away at college. That was one major reason why the family came to the United States, so their children could have a better education.

Many of the families in the complex were related to one another. Samiya's two cousins lived downstairs. If Toby Frost asked around, somebody would probably tell him about the apartment complex where so many Iraqi families lived. But Bijan hoped it would take time.

Bijan and Elie went upstairs to the

apartment where Samiya lived. They rang the bell.

"What are you doing here?" Samiya asked when she opened the door. Her parents weren't home yet.

"Samiya, we have problems. This guy—Toby Frost—he's really mad. He thinks you're telling people that he and his friends attacked you that night. He wants to talk to you, Samiya, and I'm afraid he could get violent," Bijan said.

"What?" Samiya gasped. Her lower lip trembled. "I never talked about him by name. I didn't even *know* his name. You mean he's coming here?" she asked.

"Sooner or later, he's going to find you, Samiya," Bijan said. "You need protection. If you really think Frost and his friends were the ones who attacked you, you need to go to the police."

Tears filled Samiya's eyes. She sank so deeply into the big sofa that it seemed to swallow her up. "I . . . I . . . miss Faisel so much. I cannot bear it. He will get tired of waiting for me, and he will find another girl to marry, and then I will have lost him forever. How can my parents be so cruel to keep us from each other?" Samiya sobbed.

Bijan and Elie looked at one another in confusion. Finally Bijan said, "This isn't about Faisel right now, Samiya. You need protection from that guy Frost . . . "

Samiya shook her head violently. "He didn't do it. He did not attack me," she said.

"Then who did, do you know?" Bijan asked softly.

"Nobody," the girl said so quietly that the boys barely heard it. Suddenly, Bijan realized what had happened.

"The rock that hit our house . . . the notes . . . " he said. "It was you?"

"I thought if my parents realized how much everybody hates all us Iraqis, they would take me home . . . to Faisel. I thought if you and Sami were also bothered, they would need no more proof," Samiya sobbed. "I meant no harm. I just wanted to go home to the boy I love."

Bijan and Elie stayed with Samiya until her parents got home. They tried to comfort her, but she would not be comforted. Then, finally, when her mother and father and her cousins came, the boys left.

As Bijan walked up his own driveway that night, he decided he would ask his mother to make some baklava. He would offer his apologies to Jeff Tomlinson and give him the baklava as a peace offering.

Bijan thought it might not work. But then again it might. Mother's baklava had great powers.